One morning the twins, George and Hollie, were getting ready to go out.

"Where are we going?" George asked.

"To the shops. It's a very special day," replied Mummy.

"Is it our birthday?" asked George.

"No," laughed Daddy. "We're going to buy you both potties and some big girl and boy pants."

"Yippee!" shouted the twins.

The twins sang, "We're going to get a potty!
We're going to get a potty!"

George stopped singing and wondered, "Mummy, what is a potty?"

"A Potty is a very special toilet that helps little girls and boys
learn to have a wee and a poo like a grown up," replied Mummy.

Both twins were worried about what this special toilet would be. Hollie imagined a huge toilet bowl that she could fall into. George imagined a really scary angry toilet.

"But we have nappies for that!" said Hollie.

"You're both getting too big for nappies," replied Daddy. "Don't worry it isn't scary. You'll see."

At the shop the twins asked if they could
choose their own potties.

"Can I have the ladybug one?" asked Hollie.

"Can I have the bumblebee one?" asked George.

"Of course," said Mummy.

"Good choice," said Daddy. "Those are both magic potties."

George and Hollie's eyes lit up.

"Magic how?" gasped George.

"You'll see later," said Mummy. "Now we have to get some special pants."

George and Hollie, new potties in hand, excitedly ran over to the pants' section and picked out their favourite pairs.

The twins proudly carried their potties into the house. "What do we do now?" asked George.

Mummy showed the twins their special charts.

"You have to wait until you need a wee or a poo," replied Daddy.

"If you use the potty, then you get a special sticker for your chart!"

"I'm not sure that I'm going to get a sticker," said George sadly.

"Why?" asked Mummy.

"Because I've just wet myself!" cried George.

Mummy picked up George.
"That's ok. Accidents happen.
Don't be sad."

Later that day Hollie needed
to have a wee.

"How do I do it?" asked Hollie.

"Just pull down the special pants,
sit on the potty and go!"
replied Daddy.
"Remember, it's magic!"

Hollie's puppy came to life,
ran up to her and shouted,
"You can do it Hollie!"
Hollie managed to
have a wee in the potty.

"I did it Mummy, I did it!"

said Hollie excitedly. Mummy took Hollie to wash her hands.

**Mummy let Hollie pick
a sticker for her chart.**

Later that day the twins went out to play.

"Why do we need our potties in the garden?" asked George.

"In case we need to use them of course," replied Hollie.

"Uh oh!" said Hollie, realising
she needed to have a wee.

She pulled down her pants,
sat on the potty, and began to shrink.

Hollie shrank down to the size of an insect.

Hollie's ladybug potty flew over to the flowers.

Hollie stopped at the flowers and began to smell them.
A bumblebee flew in close to her.

"Hello Mr Bumblebee!"
said Hollie.

"Hello there little girl!
What's your name?"
said the bumblebee excitedly.

"Hollie," she replied.

"Why does your brother look so sad?
He looks like he would be
having much more fun here with us!"
said the bumblebee.

"He can't. His potty isn't magic
yet," replied Hollie.

"Well, then maybe you need
to encourage him a little bit!"
suggested the bumblebee.

"Good idea!" answered Hollie.
She flew back towards George.

Hollie grew back to life size.

"George! Guess what just happened?
I flew to..." Hollie started saying.

However, she was distracted. She noticed
she'd done a poo in her potty.

"Mummy, I did it! I flew all around the garden, met a bee and I did a poo!" said Hollie.

"Wow, good girl Hollie! Time for another sticker!" replied Mummy.

George looked sad.

"What's wrong George?" asked Mummy.

"My potty isn't magic like Hollie's. It isn't fair. I'll never get a sticker," sighed George.

"It can be. The bee told me!" said Hollie.

It was time for bed, so George and Hollie had to go on their potties. George wanted a sticker so much, but nothing happened.

"Come on George, it's really important to go before bed," said Daddy.

"Remember, its magic!" said Hollie.

George closed his eyes.

George opened his eyes. He was in space. His toy train appeared.

"I bet you can't catch me!"
said the train and it choo chooed away.

George chased it through
the stars excited.

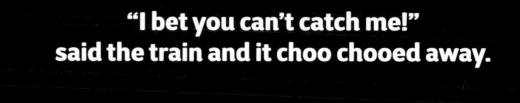

George was back in the bathroom and realised he had done a wee.

"You did it! Well done George!" said Daddy.

"Do I get a sticker now?" asked George.

"Of course you do!" laughed Daddy.

George picked the perfect
sticker for his chart.

The next morning was bright and sunny.

As George and Hollie had been so good
using their new potties, Mummy took them to
the beach for a special treat.

They played happily at the beach all day and of course
didn't forget to bring their magic potties.

It was time to go to bed.

"Night night!" said George

"Night night!" said Hollie.

George and Hollie went to sleep and never had
any problems going to the potty again.